This book belongs to:

_____

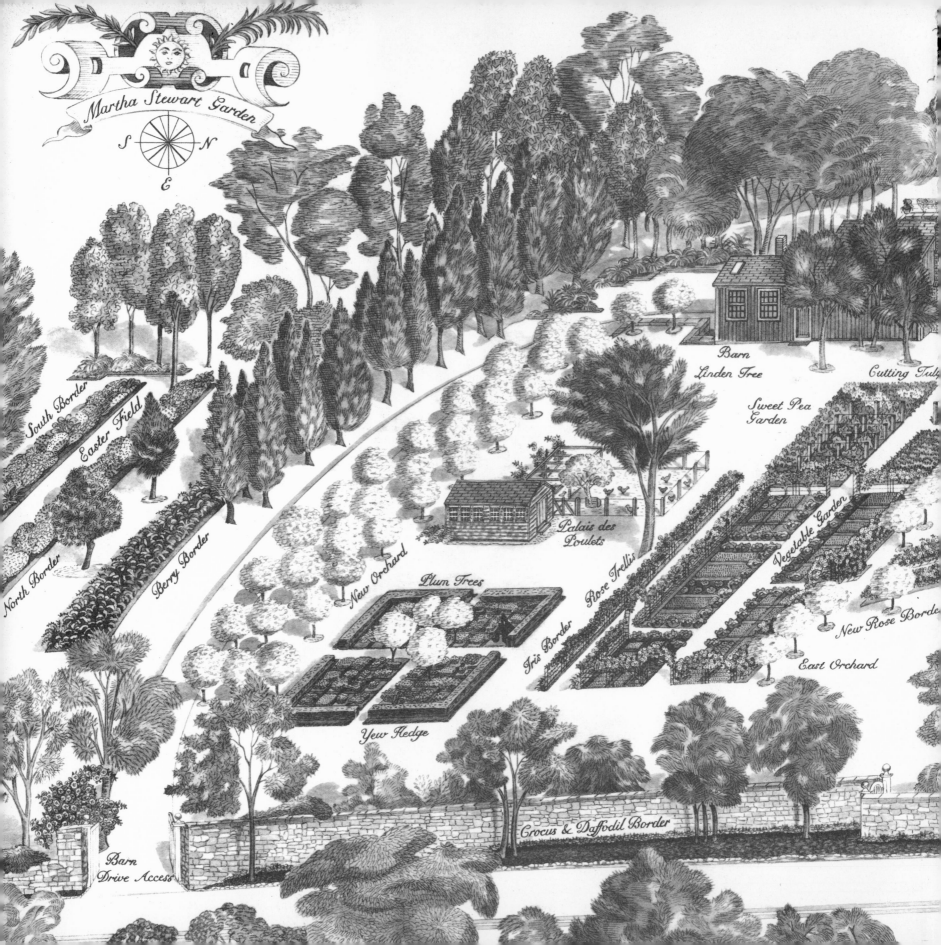

Martha Stewart Garden

S   N
E

South Border

Easter Field

North Border

Berry Border

New Orchard

Plum Trees

Yew Hedge

Iris Border

Rose Trellis

Palais des Poulets

Barn

Linden Tree

Cutting Tuli

Sweet Pea Garden

Vegetable Garden

New Rose Borde

East Orchard

Crocus & Daffodil Border

Barn
Drive Access

Dream BIG Little Pig!

KRISTI YAMAGUCHI

Illustrated by Tim Bowers

sourcebooks
jabberwocky

Published by Sourcebooks Jabberwocky, an imprint of Sourcebooks, Inc.
P.O. Box 4410, Naperville, Illinois 60567-4410
(630) 961-3900
Fax: (630) 961-2168
www.jabberwockykids.com

Library of Congress Cataloging-in-Publication data is on file with the publisher.

Source of Production: Bang Printing, Brainerd, MN, USA
Date of Production: April 2011
Run number: 14983

Printed and bound in the United States of America.
BG 10 9 8 7 6 5 4 3

Poppy was a pig.

A pot-bellied, waddling, toddling pig.

She was a pig with dreams. And she

was a pig who dreamed big!

She wanted to be a star.

Poppy had always dreamed of
being a posh prima ballerina.

She tried out for Swan Lake, a famous ballet.

But Poppy was not graceful. In fact,

she was quite clumsy.

"Follow your dreams!" said Poppy's mother, who loved her no matter what. "You go, girl!" said Poppy's grandparents, who were her biggest fans. "Dream big, pig!" said Poppy's best friend, Emma, who was always there for her.

"Dancing is just not for you," said
the people in charge of the ballet.
"Try something else!"

So Poppy tried out for Singing Stars,
a popular chorus competition.
She had always dreamed
of being a soulful singer.

But Poppy sang off-key. And to be honest,
she couldn't really carry a tune.

"You go, girl!" said
Poppy's grandparents.

"Follow your
dreams!" said
Poppy's mother.

"Dream big, pig!"
said Emma.

"Singing is just not for you," said the people in charge of the competition. "Try something else!"

So Poppy tried out for Supermodel Search.
She had always dreamed of being a big-time
splashy supermodel.

But Poppy
was not very glitzy
or glittery, and she even
tripped on her fancy gown.

"Follow your dreams!" said Poppy's mother.

"You go, girl!" said Poppy's grandparents.

"Dream big, pig!" said Emma.

"Modeling is just not for you," said the
people in charge of the search.
"Try something else!"

But Poppy didn't know what else to try.

And as she wandered through New Pork City,
she began to wonder if her dreams
would really come true.

Poppy was about to give up when she
heard her mother say, "Just follow your heart.
Remember, we love you no matter what."
And her grandparents cheer, "We're your biggest fans!"
And her best friend, Emma, squeal,
"We're here for you!"

Poppy smiled. She knew
just what to do!

When Poppy thought about all the things she truly loved—her
friends and family were at the top of the list! So, the next day,
Poppy invited Emma for a "pig's day out" in the park.

While giggling and strolling along, they spotted an ice rink.
Poppy and Emma watched the skaters skimming and spinning,
swooping and swizzling on the ice. Poppy realized it was the
most beautiful sight she had ever seen.
Her heart danced with joy!

Emma saw a twinkle in Poppy's eye and
high-fived her friend. "Dream big, pig!" she cheered.
So Poppy waddled and toddled right up to the
teacher and said, "I'd like to be
a spectacular ice-skating star."

"A pig on ice?" the teacher
pondered. "Honey, I don't
know if that's possible."

"Anything's possible,"
responded Poppy. "I believe
in dreaming big!"

The teacher shrugged. "As you wish," she said.
"We'll see if the pig's got pizzazz."

Poppy laced up her
skates. She slipped and
slid all over the ice.
She fell.

But, this time…

...Poppy got up.

Over and over and over, she
shuffled and stumbled and
fumbled and fell.

But by the time the rink closed for the night,
Poppy was skating more than she was falling.
And it felt like…magic!

Poppy returned to the rink the very next day.
Her cheeks were pink with winter
wind and excitement.

She was so happy gliding and
sliding and tumbling and bumbling
on the ice, she didn't even notice
that she wasn't perfect.

And nobody else did either.

Now, a most persistent pig, Poppy learned to twirl
and swirl and to do dips and lunges and splits.
Poppy learned to do jumps and spirals and lifts.

Before she knew it, more and more
skaters stopped to watch Poppy practice—she
was quite a sight! She even had her picture
on the front page of the newspaper.
Poppy felt like a star!

Some of her fans made T-shirts
that read "FOLLOW YOUR DREAMS!" Others
wore hats that said "DREAM BIG, PIG!" And
tote bags declared "YOU GO, GIRL!"
Poppy's dreams had come true!

Time went by, but Poppy didn't stop dreaming.
One day, she decided to be a pilot. She wanted
to parachute and be the first sky-diving pig.
"When pigs fly!" said the other pilots.
But they did not know Poppy.
She was a pig who dreamed big.

To Mommy's Angels— Keara and Emma, you give me more joy than I can ever express. This is for you both in hopes that you will always dream big! I love you to infinity...Mom

Acknowledgments

To Linda Oatman High, it was so amazing collaborating ideas with you. Poppy is certainly someone who is inspiring and positive, and you helped bring her to life. A heartfelt thank-you to you for writing this book with me. It's been such an honor.
—Kristi

To Rubin, an encouraging voice when I'm dreaming big.
—T.B.